SCOTNOTES 10

Robin Jenkins's
THE CONE-GATHERERS

SCOTNOTES
Number 10

Robin Jenkins's

The Cone-Gatherers

Iain Crichton Smith

Association for Scottish Literary Studies 1995

Published by
Association for Scottish Literary Studies
Scottish Literature
7 University Gardens
University of Glasgow
Glasgow G12 8QH
www.asls.org.uk

ASLS is a registered charity no. SC006535

First published 1995

Revised 2013

A CIP catalogue for this title is available from the British Library

ISBN 978-0-948877-26-1

The Association for Scottish Literary Studies acknowledges the support of Creative Scotland towards the publication of this book.

Printed by Bell and Bain Ltd, Glasgow

CONTENTS

NOTE ON REFERENCES

The page references given in the text are to the Canongate edition of *The Cone-Gatherers,* Edinburgh, 2012.

1. INTRODUCTION

Robin Jenkins was born in Cambuslang in 1912 and educated at Hamilton Academy and Glasgow University. For a time he taught English in Glasgow and at Dunoon, Argyll. In 1956 he went to Afghanistan to teach, from where he went to Spain and then to British North Borneo (now part of Malaysia). He returned to Dunoon where he has since made his home.

Some of his books, such as *The Cone-Gatherers,* are set in Scotland: others are set abroad. For instance *Dust on the Paw* is set in Afghanistan.

During the Second World War (1939–1945) Jenkins was a conscientious objector and worked in forestry.

Jenkins has written:

> As a consequence of my having been brought up in a small community I have never been at ease living in a large city and few of my novels have urban settings. As a university student I used to go hiking in the Highlands, often alone, which was foolish from the point of view of safety but valuable in that it compelled me to feel closer to nature than I would have if I had had companions to talk to. Also, walking through a desolate glen for hours at a stretch, often in mist and rain, with only birds and sheep and deer for company, was a good way of getting to know not only the presences all around me but also, more importantly, myself. Novelists who seek to study the virtues and vices of humanity find them all most readily in themselves.
>
> I did once gather cones, in an autumnal wood, in wartime, but none of my workmates was anything like Neil and Calum, and there was no sinister Duror skulking among the trees. They all came out of my imagination.[1]

Certainly Jenkins is the kind of novelist who explores 'the virtues and vices' of people and in fact goes further than that as he explores good and evil as well. It may be true, as he says, that we find the virtues and vices of humanity most readily in ourselves. It may be true that everyone has the capacity to be a Duror. But Jenkins is also careful to say that these characters came out of his imagination. He did not actually see these people in the world around him. But it is also true that such people are not impossible to imagine. In the same introduction from which I have quoted, Jenkins refers to the General Strike of 1926 in which the miners were involved (Jenkins was born and brought up in a mining village). He saw

> [...] miners armed with clubs ready to attack any bus driver who tried to drive through [...] I have never forgotten the anger on these miners' faces. They were men I had often seen sitting in the sun chatting or playing cards [...] I had been given a glimpse of the fury and resentment below the surface, not only in them but in all of us. I am sure that experience helped me to create the character of Duror in *The Cone-Gatherers*.[2]

What Jenkins is saying is that hatred is not an alien concept. Duror is not a monster whom we cannot understand. 'Fury and resentment' have partly made him what he is. In the same way as the miners were incited to hatred by the constriction of their lives, Duror too turned to hatred through the constriction of his.

2. SUMMARY

Chapters 1–4

In these chapters we are introduced first of all to the brothers Neil and Calum who are high in the trees gathering cones. So much of the wood is being used for war purposes that it will have to be re-seeded with these cones. Calum is absolutely at home in the trees, helping his brother down from the trees, though on the ground he is clumsy because of his deformity.

We find out that Calum is very compassionate to animals and sensitive to their pain and has released some rabbits from the traps which Duror, the keeper, has set. For this reason, Duror hates the two brothers (Calum in particular) and wants them out of the wood. They come across a snared rabbit with both its front paws broken. Calum cannot bring himself to put it out of its misery.

Duror has been watching them in 'an icy sweat of hatred' (11), his gun aimed at the hunchback Calum. The wood was his refuge but now he thinks it is polluted by this 'freak'. Also he says that the two brothers are defiling with refuse the area around their hut.

He kills the rabbit with one blow and then makes his way to the brothers' dirty hut, where he spies on them obsessively. Throughout these early pages the dominant emotion is Duror's savage hatred for the brothers, whom he calls sub-human.

Duror then meets Dr Matheson, the local doctor, who seems more interested in his food, or lack of it, than in anything else. Because of the war, Spam (cheap processed pork) is the main meat and the doctor, who has clearly been used to rich food such as venison, and good whisky, is not very happy. However, he is a shrewd man and we do find out his opinion of Duror, whom he suspects of hiding seething emotions behind an apparently calm surface. He senses a fanatical nature behind the composure (19).

After meeting the doctor, Duror goes home to a desperately unhappy domestic situation. His wife, Peggy, is grossly fat and bedridden, and in her own way deformed. She is described as having 'great wobbling masses of pallid fat' (25). It is clear that his life is a dreadfully constricting one, with a bedridden wife and a dour hostile mother-in-law, Mrs Lochie, who accuses him of speaking more often to his dogs than to her daughter.

She gives him the news that the mistress of the estate, Lady Runcie-Campbell, wants a deer hunt organised for her brother who is on leave (32).

The prospective deer hunt allows Duror to concoct a plot in which the two brothers will be drafted in as beaters. He knows that because of his sensitivity to pain in animals, Calum is likely to disgrace himself and Lady Runcie-Campbell may dismiss the two brothers from her estate.

The following morning we are introduced to Roderick, Lady Runcie-Campbell's son, who is rather a clumsy boy, and Sheila his sister, as well as Captain Forgan, their uncle. We discover that Duror thinks of deer as vermin (40), while his mistress, though willing to hunt and kill them, regards them as beautiful.

There is a brief interlude with Duror and Mrs Morton, the buxom cook-housekeeper, from which we gather that Duror is sexually repressed. When he brings up the subject of the brothers, Mrs Morton shows no hostility to them but Duror is quite happy to tell lies about them, and in fact suggests that Calum is a sexual pervert and dangerous to young girls like Sheila. He says that he has seen Calum exposing himself (47).

In a discussion with Lady Runcie-Campbell, Duror suggests that, because of a shortage of beaters, the two brothers should be used. She asks Mr Tulloch, the head forester, for permission to use them, and he agrees. However, Tulloch phones again and says that Calum has scruples about being a beater. After consultation with Duror, she insists that the brothers join the hunt, her imperious aristocratic nature for the moment overcoming her Christian compassion. Later, however, she does propose a compromise, that only Neil should be used, but Duror will have none of it. Thus, the fateful deer hunt goes ahead (61).

Chapters 5–9

The two brothers who are up in the trees see Duror approaching. Then to their astonishment he begins to climb the ladder up to where the brothers are. To his own humiliation, however, Duror suffers from fear and dizziness and has to give up climbing. From far below, he tells them that Lady Runcie-Campbell wants them as beaters in a deer-drive that afternoon (69–70). Neil is enraged on behalf of Calum. Meanwhile, Duror is ashamed that he cannot do what Calum can so easily do, that is, climb trees.

Neil insists that they will not take part in the deer hunt. He says that Calum has been excused deer hunts in the forest: why should he have to do them here? He says that they are 'free men' and not at the beck and call of Lady Runcie-Campbell. He also feels that Tulloch has betrayed them. However, Calum says that he will do his best (74).

We are then introduced to some minor characters in the book: Harry, the gardener apprentice, Betty, the gum-chewing landgirl, Erchie Graham, an old handyman, and Charlie, a labourer. These, and in particular Graham, lighten an otherwise sombre narrative with some humour (75–76).

They are all startled to see Duror rising up near them and shouting 'Peggy'. Duror has had a nightmare in which he sees his wife being attacked by thrushes. At this point the two brothers appear (78). Neil has conceded that they will have to take part in the deer hunt. Graham tells them that, when they hear the guns, they should lie down as there is a man in the hunt who is as blind as a mole. All this time, Duror's subordinates find his behaviour odd. His speech seems blurred and, although usually tidy, he has not shaved (81).

When the drive begins, Calum flees with the fleeing deer and flings himself on a wounded one as if to comfort it while it drags him along and its blood stains him. Duror thereupon rushes on the deer and savagely cuts its throat (86). He seems caught up in a murderous frenzy and after it he collapses and begins to speak his wife's name. Lady Runcie-Campbell tells him he is sick and should see a doctor. Meanwhile, Tulloch talks to the brothers and says that though Calum is being blamed for the fiasco of the hunt, he will stand up for the two brothers (91–92).

Lady Runcie-Campbell is furious with the two brothers and says that they must go. Her son Roderick, however, who admires the brothers for their ability to climb tall trees, defends them, and so does Tulloch. When Captain Forgan tells his sister that he has not been offended by their behaviour she agrees that they can stay (96).

On Saturday, the brothers, as usual, go to the town of Lendrick by bus. They are made welcome in the local shops and the café. We find out, however, that the conscientious objectors who work in the forest are not so welcome in the town: and Neil to his own disgust treats them in the same way as the townspeople do (108).

Lady Runcie-Campbell has meanwhile made an appointment for Duror to see the doctor and runs him into Lendrick where she and her two children are going to the pictures. Roderick suggests that they offer Neil and Calum a lift back since otherwise they will have to walk, but Sheila strongly objects (113).

Duror visits the doctor, bringing a gift of venison with Lady Runcie-Campbell's compliments. There is, it turns out, nothing wrong with him physically, though the doctor suspects that emotionally and mentally all is not well. We find out from his interrogation of Duror that Duror was only twenty-eight years old when his wife was stricken and that they had only been married three years. The doctor concludes by saying that since Duror is not a religious man he must simply endure his burden (124).

When Duror leaves the surgery he goes to the hotel bar where there are a number of local workers and the two brothers. Four English soldiers enter and one of them tells a joke about a fighter pilot and an ape. Then noticing Calum, he profusely apologises (132). One of the people in the pub says after the brothers have left that he has heard that their mother committed suicide after Calum's birth and that she came from one of the islands, perhaps Mull.

Chapters 10–12

Lady Runcie-Campbell pays her usual charitable visit to Peggy who fawns on her because she is an aristocrat. She muses about how Christianity can be reconciled with rank, and we learn something about her husband Colin, who is unthinkingly anti-egalitarian, and her father, who had been a judge, who believed in practical charity and who had taught his grandson Roderick to be friendly to his social inferiors.

When she returns from the visit to Duror's wife she tells Roderick that he ought to be out in the sunshine. He suggests that he might go to the beach and asks Mrs Morton for a cake to take with him (140). She warns him not to go near the cone-gatherers, remembering what Duror has told her, but he intends to visit them and give them the cake as a form of reparation. An imaginative boy, he thinks of his journey through the wood as a sort of pilgrimage through a realm of magic and terror (143). When he approaches the hut he sees Duror spying there and he himself goes into hiding (144). He wonders whether Duror has gone mad and thinks of him as evil. When eventually Duror departs he leaves the cake to be devoured by insects. He feels that somehow Duror has defiled the wood.

A storm of thunder and lightning and rain arises while the brothers are in the trees. A light in the sky reminds Calum of heaven, where he thinks his mother is, but Neil, who is not religious, tries to disillusion him (151). Because of the intensity of the storm, Neil decides that they should go to the beach hut which is forbidden to them. Once inside they light a fire and rummage among the old toys which once belonged to Lady Runcie-Campbell's children. However, as they are making themselves comfortable, she and her children come into the hut to shelter from the rain (156). She is very angry when she finds the two brothers there and tells them to leave. Sheila is, as usual, mocking and pitiless but Roderick becomes ominously silent as if disapproving of his mother's action. Lady Runcie-Campbell and Sheila make good use of the fire that the brothers have lit (159).

Tulloch learns from both Neil and Lady Runcie-Campbell what has happened and goes to see the brothers. From a distance, he catches sight of Neil on his knees conscientiously gathering beech seed and suddenly realises how old he looks. Neil tells Tulloch that Lady Runcie-Campbell was more concerned about her dog than about the two of them. Tulloch decides that he will take them from the wood and back to their previous employment and replace them with two conscientious objectors (164–65). Neil volunteers to stay till the end of the week and, if Lady Runcie-Campbell apologises to Calum and himself, longer (167).

The incident of the hut has shown again the vast distance between privilege and deprivation: and it emphasises to the brothers that Tulloch is their best and most helpful friend.

Chapters 13–16

Lady Runcie-Campbell and Roderick have an argument about her attitude to the cone-gatherers and he accuses her of unfairness in sending them out of the hut. She says that he must assert his inherited position in the world. She also decides that she is going to send them away (174).

She phones Duror to get his co-operation in making the brothers leave. Mrs Lochie answers the phone and says that her son-in-law has come in with a doll, an incident which she finds disturbing (178–79). Tulloch visits the brothers and informs them that they can leave the wood shortly (182). He meets Roderick and tells him this and he seems downcast by the news.

Tulloch goes to see Lady Runcie-Campbell and tells her of his decision and that he intends to replace the brothers with conscientious objectors. She is not very happy about this, thinking of conscientious objectors as cowards (188–89).

While they are talking Duror appears. He produces a doll which he says he found in the brothers' hut, a doll which indeed Calum had taken from the beach house when they were sheltering from the storm and which he took with him in order to repair its broken leg. Duror wishes to create what Lady Runcie-Campbell calls a 'filthy mystery' (191) out of this but fails of his purpose, though he also makes the most loathsome accusations against Calum. She asks him if he has gone mad and orders him to go home. However, when he says that he has work to do she tells him to go and do it (193).

After he has left, his behaviour and particularly his hatred of Calum are discussed by Tulloch and Lady Runcie-Campbell, Tulloch suggesting various theories about them.

When Lady Runcie-Campbell parts from Tulloch and has been in the house a while, Mrs Morton comes to tell her that Harry is in the kitchen with a story that Roderick is trapped high in a tree (199). Neither he nor Graham is able to climb high enough to bring him down. She goes to the tree herself and shouts reassuringly to Roderick, who does not reply. She then sends Graham for the two brothers (204).

However, when Graham delivers the order from Lady Runcie-Campbell, Neil refuses to help and says that he and Calum are not her servants. She must come and make the request in person (209).

On his way back from the recalcitrant Neil, Graham encounters Duror and tells him of his failed mission. Duror stalks away in the direction of the brothers without speaking (212–13).

When Graham arrives back at the tree, Roderick is still trapped in it. Graham tells Lady Runcie-Campbell what Neil has said to him, that they will come only if she personally pleads for them to do so (215). He also tells her about Duror.

She then decides that she will go and see the brothers. As she approaches them she hears the sound of a gun (219). She sees Duror walking away and then she comes upon Calum's body hanging in a tree. He has been shot by Duror. As she watches Neil trying to reach his brother she hears another shot and knows that Duror has killed himself (219). Meanwhile, she hears Sheila shouting that Roderick has been helped down from the tree by Harry. The book ends as she goes down on her knees near the blood and the cones which are falling from the bag that Calum was filling.

3. STRUCTURE

The novel is structured in a fairly simple manner. There are three main events which give it clarity. The first is the deer hunt, the second the storm scene, and the third Roderick's entrapment in the tree.

The deer hunt is used by Duror to drive the brothers out of the wood by means of Calum's known hatred of cruelty. He calculates that Calum will do something which will offend Lady Runcie-Campbell for whose brother the deer hunt has been organised. Calum does in fact turn the deer hunt into a fiasco and Lady Runcie-Campbell is furious. However, when Roderick intercedes on behalf of the brothers, and her brother remains neutral, and Tulloch is on their side, she changes her mind and lets them stay (93–94). Thus, Duror fails in his plot.

A sub-plot used by Duror is his hint to Mrs Morton, the doctor, and Lady Runcie-Campbell that Calum is a sexual pervert. This again does not succeed since by this time Duror's own behaviour has become eccentric (47, 121, 192).

The storm scene is important because it brings the brothers into direct confrontation with Lady Runcie-Campbell (156–57). This time, because of the heavy rain, thunder and lightning, they break into the beach hut on Neil's initiative, though the hut is forbidden territory to them. Lady Runcie-Campbell is again furious when she finds them there and orders them out. Roderick is silent when she asks him whether she has been unfair: Sheila, the daughter, is triumphant in the tradition of the class-conscious aristocrat.

As a direct result of this incident Roderick leaves the house and climbs a tree from which he cannot get down. None of Lady Runcie-Campbell's servants are able to help so she sends peremptorily for the brothers. Neil refuses to come unless she herself pleads with them in person (209). The messenger, Graham, on his way back with the news of Neil's inflexible refusal, meets Duror whom he informs of Neil's attitude. Without a word, Duror sets off in the direction of the brothers. Lady Runcie-Campbell, hearing of the meeting with Duror as well as of Neil's ultimatum, decides to go and see the brothers herself. As she approaches she hears a gunshot (219). Duror has shot Calum and then killed himself. This brings the book to an end.

In each event Lady Runcie-Campbell is involved, though it is not she but Duror who initiates the evil in the book by means of the deer hunt.

The structure is strengthened by the fact that the action is generally confined to the wood, except for the visit by the brothers to Lendrick. This suggests that the book is intended to be a tragedy in the classical Greek sense with a fixed locality, a short period of time, and a sense of inevitability. This little tragedy is set against the wider violence of the Second World War whose echoes we hear in the wood. Thus, we might get the impression that because of the tragedy in the wood and the wider tragedy of the war, there is in man a violence which he cannot control. However, one of the functions of Calum is to show us, by the goodness of his nature, that there is an alternative. The ending, which remains to be discussed, is strangely hopeful, in spite of the violence of which we hear so much.

Certain images too link the action. One of these is the cones. The brothers are gathering cones to re-seed the forest. When Roderick climbs the tree it is clearly in imitation of the brothers, since he is carrying a bag for collecting cones (203). Then at the very end the cones fall from Calum's bag as he hangs in the tree, dead (219). In general, the cones are symbols for regeneration. Another image is that of the monkey or ape which is applied to Calum (132). Thus, on one level, Calum represents man's descent from the monkey as in the theory of Darwin but, on the other, he is compared to Christ with the image of his being crucified in the tree. Such images link the narrative in an interesting manner and tighten the structure of the book.

4. THE PERIOD

The period during which the action takes place is the Second World War (1939–1945). Britain was fighting against Nazi Germany, which was led by the dictator Adolf Hitler.

On the very first page we read of a destroyer and aeroplanes. The cones themselves are being used to re-seed the forest because much of the wood is being used for war purposes.

In the first meeting between Duror and Dr Matheson the latter is complaining of the fact that he has to eat Spam, a meat which was used because other meats were not available or were strictly rationed (19).

When Duror arrives at his house and we encounter his wife Peggy and his mother-in-law, the wireless (radio) is on and Stalingrad is mentioned (27). Stalingrad was a city in Russia which had to suffer a protracted and cruel siege by the Germans in 1942. However, it did not surrender and its heroic resistance marked a turning point in the war.

Lady Runcie-Campbell's brother, Captain Forgan, is home for a few days' leave and it is he who asks for the deer hunt.

In the café in Lendrick, Calum and Neil see the Ardmore workers enter. They are conscientious objectors, that is, people who, often on religious grounds, would not take part in actual fighting but would do non-military jobs such as would benefit the country, e.g. forestry or farming. Such men were not popular and were often accused of cowardice. The villagers of Lendrick are not friendly with them and Lady Runcie-Campbell, with her traditional aristocratic values, does not care for them. In the hotel bar in Lendrick we meet four English soldiers, one of whom tells a joke which he apologises for later, as he thinks it might have offended Calum (132). We learn that Tulloch's brother has been killed at Dunkirk, a major disaster for Britain's forces on the Continent in 1940, when they were driven into the sea by the Germans and had to be rescued by the Navy and civilian boats drafted in for the occasion.

Mrs Morton's son Alec is in the Merchant Navy. Duror himself would like to be in the war but they will not take him. He is in the Home Guard instead, an organisation in which civilians were given some training in weaponry in order to defend the country if the Germans landed.

There is a reference by Duror to the fact that 'the Germans were putting idiots and cripples to death in gas chambers' (15). This refers to the Nazi ideal of the Aryan as the perfect human being, which meant that Jews were murdered as also were the handicapped and the physically deformed. Gypsies and homosexuals were other groups attacked.

One front on which the war was fought was the North African one. Commanders such as Montgomery fought there, as did the famous German general, Rommel. This explains the reference to Captain Forgan, that shortly after his leave he would be in the African desert (38).

This background of war serves useful purposes to the author. On the one hand, as has already been mentioned, it suggests that evil is to be found among human beings everywhere and is not confined to the wood. Also, and very important, it means that Lady Runcie-Campbell's husband is away from the estate. If he had been there he would have dealt summarily with the two brothers and would not have suffered from the ethical indecisions that his wife suffered from. Furthermore, the war being fought against an unjust Nazi regime fuels Neil's ideals of equality and independence from authority. Neil is much more rebellious than Calum and feels deeply the disparity between people such as himself and Lady Runcie-Campbell. He feels that when the war is over a new social regime will be instituted which will be much fairer.

5. CHARACTERS

In order of appearance in the book, the characters are Calum and Neil, Duror, Dr Matheson, Mrs Lochie, Peggy Duror, Captain Forgan, Roderick, Sheila, Mrs Morton, Lady Runcie-Campbell, Mr Tulloch, Harry, Betty, Erchie Graham. Many of this cast are minor characters. We will begin with the major characters.

Duror

Duror is a forester. His wife Peggy is bedridden and has become vastly obese. Her mother, Mrs Lochie, stays in the house to look after her, but is not very fond of Duror, who she considers does not pay enough attention to her daughter (24–35). Thus, Duror's domestic situation is unhappy. Indeed, he has tried to get into the army, probably to escape from his wretchedness.

He hates the two brothers, especially Calum who removes animals from the traps that he has set. This hatred which leads to such dreadful consequences is worth examining in detail. We are told that:

> Since childhood Duror had been repelled by anything living that had an imperfection or deformity or lack: a cat with three legs had roused pity in others, but in him an ungovernable disgust. (13)

Clearly, too, his monstrously fat wife, in her own way deformed, disgusts him and we are told that 'Her wheedling voice reminded him of the hunchback's' (25).

The question of Duror's hatred of Calum is examined by Tulloch at great length in conversation with Lady Runcie-Campbell:

> [...] why had Duror taken a spite against Calum? [...] It could be the whole man's disgust at the deformed man, unreasonable and instinctive: he had seen, for instance, crows mobbing one that had a broken wing. Or it could be that Duror resented their intrusion into the wood: again in nature animals had

> their own hunting grounds and chased off trespassers. Or it could be that the dislike was simply inexplicable: once he had known a horse that showed its teeth in anger every time it saw a certain man; and that man had certainly never treated it cruelly. (194)

This question of Duror's hatred of Calum is an interesting one. On the one hand, we know that others such as the Lendrick villagers and the conscientious objectors accept Calum quite easily without any hostility. However, as noted previously, the Nazis were willing in the service of a false ideal to put 'imperfect' people such as hunchbacks to death.

Duror in the service of his hatred is willing to set a trap for Calum at the deer hunt, and he also tells lies about him, that he is a sexual pervert.

There seems to be little question that mixed up in his hatred is his wife's deformity, of which Calum reminds him continually. But also Calum, though physically ugly, is facially beautiful, and there shines from him a light of goodness. It is perhaps this more than anything that Duror cannot bear, the manner in which Calum responds to his own deformity, without hatred or bitterness.

Duror is not a monster who is beyond understanding. We can understand him and sometimes even pity him as we learn his history, and also as we get our last glimpse of him through the eyes of Lady Runcie-Campbell:

> He was walking away among the pine trees with so infinite a desolation in his every step that it was this memory of him [...] which was to torment her sleep for months. (219)

This occurs just after he has shot Calum and before he shoots himself.

At this point Duror becomes a figure of evil who has destroyed goodness, and the author describes Calum's death in terms of the crucifixion of Christ. Thus, from being a figure of twisted bitterness, Duror takes on a greater dimension, and we remember that Judas who betrayed Christ also went away by himself and committed suicide.

Calum

Calum, as we have seen, is the innocent victim of Duror's malignity. His physical appearance, apart from his beautiful angelic face, is ugly. We are told that he looks like a monkey, that he shuffles along, hands close to the ground, and his head seems to have no neck while his shoulders are grotesquely humped (78). It is not only on Duror that his appearance has a repellent effect. Betty, the landgirl, says that he 'fair gies me the creeps' (79) and Harry remarks that he once saw a jungle picture which had a pet ape in it and that it looked just like Calum (79).

In the scene in the bar in Lendrick this resemblance to an ape is referred to when the English soldier tells a story about a fighter pilot who kept a pet ape. Many in the pub were embarrassed, for they 'had already associated the little hunchback with the monkey in the silly story' (132).

It is the contrast between Calum's angelic face and his deformed grotesque body which particularly angers and agitates Duror. Calum is a being composed it seems of angel and ape.

Sitting high in the trees he seems perfectly at home, 'his sunburnt face was alert and beautiful with trust' (2). In this he contrasts with his brother Neil who is not quite so much at ease in the trees and sometimes has to be helped down. Neither Duror himself nor Roderick can climb high trees without getting into trouble. On the ground, however, Calum stumbles continually.

He identifies himself with the animals and birds of the wood, for instance with the owl. He suffers with the victims of predators – with the deer at the deer hunt and with the rabbits caught in traps. His sensitivity is abnormal, much more so than that of his brother Neil. It is not that he has abstract ideas of right and wrong but that he yields, we are told, to instinct. Thus he does not, like his brother, have abstract notions about the unfairness of the world. Indeed, he seems continually happy.

Calum's instinctive identification with the victim allows him to be friendly with the conscientious objectors (108). In fact, he is more friendly than Neil who is more influenced by the prejudices of the society around him. Calum reacts to people and is not interested in or is perhaps not able to grasp principles such as, for instance, those which animate the conscientious objectors. Nor is he able to grasp the principles which make people hostile to them.

In short, Calum has an absolute goodness which Duror cannot tolerate.

During the storm, Calum like any animal is frightened by the thunder and lightning, and seeing a light in the sky begins to talk about heaven and his dead mother (150–51). He is like a child and believes like a child in such stories. He does not want to go into the beach hut because it is forbidden and the brothers have given a promise that they would not do so (151–52). But once inside the hut Calum begins to examine the pictures on the walls with delight, perhaps because they might have been painted by children, as indeed they had been, by Roderick and Sheila. He takes pleasure in the toys and particularly a doll with a broken leg, another victim. He wants to take the doll away in order to put a leg on it (155).

At the end of the story Calum is shot by Duror. It is Lady Runcie-Campbell who finds him. He is hanging from a tree in a twisted fashion, swinging:

> Though he smiled, he was dead. From his bag dropped a cone, and then another. There might have been more, but other drops, also singly, but faster and faster, distracted her: these were of blood. (219)

In summary, then, what kind of person is Calum? He is first of all monstrously deformed in body but angelic in face. He is good and childlike and entirely innocent. He identifies closely with victims. He is completely at home in the trees, like a monkey, but clumsy on the ground. He radiates trust and goodwill. Among the reasons Duror has for hating him is Calum's superior agility in the trees and his instinctive talent for art, for carving animals. The last scene identifies him as a Christ figure crucified on a tree, but he is also, by analogy throughout the book, ape as well. It may be that among the many things Jenkins is saying in the book is that before man came to live on the ground there was a simplicity and innocence about him which he later lost in the complexity of human action and behaviour. A defencelessness such as Calum's would not be able to survive a cunning predator like Duror. He needs help in a complex world and it is this help which his brother supplies. It is probable, as we have already said, that what Duror cannot tolerate is not so much Calum's physical ugliness as the radiance of goodness that streams from him and which Duror, caught up in the trap of his dreadful domestic circumstances, cannot possibly attain to.

Neil

Neil is quite different from Calum: he is for example more worldly-wise and aware of class differences. He says, referring to the mansion in which Lady Runcie-Campbell lives, that it has fifty rooms, each one of them bigger than the hut in which he and his brother stay. He also comments on the fact that most of these rooms are empty (4).

Unlike Calum, he is aware of the world beyond the wood and he thinks that the war is being fought for equality and for improvement in the life of the ordinary individual.

In order to survive in a world in which he has refrained from marrying in order to look after his brother, he cannot afford to be as sensitive as Calum. At the beginning of the book, he passes the stricken rabbit without noticing it and when Calum stops to release it he rushes back to shout at him: 'Are you such a child you're going to cry because a rabbit's legs are broken in a snare?' (8).

While Calum thinks of the rabbit, Neil thinks rather of the men and children who are being killed and injured in the war.

Unlike Calum, he has to think of the future. What will happen to his brother if he, Neil, dies? He is on the whole a healthy man apart from his rheumatism but, as he says, he could meet with an accident, e.g. he might get pneumonia or suffer an adder bite or fall from a tree or be cut by an axe.

Calum may live in an eternal present but practical affairs must be attended to. Groceries must be ordered so that the van can deliver them. Calum too needs a new shirt. All this Neil must do. Unlike Calum, therefore, he sees nature as essentially hostile, and the possible adder bite reflects his fear of its potential danger to his own life, which is precious not for its own sake, but for the sake of Calum.

He has grown to depend on his rights. Because he and his brother do not break branches or harm anybody he thinks that nobody should interfere with them. They are there to collect cones and nothing else; he relies on the letter of the contract. He has a keen sense of justice and fairness which is based on a wider view of the world than he has directly experienced. It is more legalistic and abstract than Calum's, which is more instinctive.

'The proud claims of honour and independence and courage made on behalf of his country at war' (100) had had an effect on him. If the war was being fought for justice, then it was being fought for people like himself and Calum.

He believes, however, that Lady Runcie-Campbell prefers her animals to them and that her dog's kennel is more luxurious than their hut. This may not be true of Lady Runcie-Campbell but Sheila certainly prefers her dog to them (114). It is interesting that the dog's name is Monty, which was the common name applied to General Montgomery who defeated the Germans in North Africa.

Unlike Calum, however, Neil is not wholeheartedly friendly to the conscientious objectors. In this he remains conventional in his attitude. He hurries past with a nod or speaks to them as briefly as possible though he knows in his heart that he is wrong in not speaking up in defence of men whom he has worked beside (108).

Unlike Calum, too, he does not believe in heaven. When Calum tells him about the light and seeing his mother in heaven, Neil ponders that there is no heaven and no merciful God (150). If it is true that his mother committed suicide after the birth of a deformed child (133) whom he has had to look after all his life, foregoing the possibility of marriage in the process (5), then one can understand why Neil does not believe in God.

It is interesting that though he is aggressive in his social ideas he does not raise his head when Lady Runcie-Campbell speaks harshly to him in the hut. 'A lifetime of frightened submissiveness' makes him keep his head down (157). But at the end of the book when Roderick is trapped in the tree he finds the courage to defy her. He tells Graham the messenger that he and his brother are not her servants and that she must come herself (209).

At the end of the book he is desperately trying to reach his brother's body. Throughout the novel he has certainly been his brother's keeper and his future looks very bleak indeed.

Lady Runcie-Campbell

Lady Runcie-Campbell is an interesting creation, an aristocrat with a conscience, though this conscience is in fact often silenced by the basic assumption common to her class that her position makes her superior to ordinary men and women.

We are told that she is very beautiful with a beauty married to 'earnestness of spirit' (50). Her father, who had been a judge, had bequeathed to her a sense of justice, even sometimes at the expense of her rank. She is a Christian though her father was not.

She would in fact have given the brothers the beach hut if it had not been for Duror and apparently she did not know the squalid nature of their accommodation (51).

In spite of her 'sentimental' feeling for the deer she finds Calum's excessive sensitivity unintelligible. She sees no problem in reconciling her Christianity with the killing of deer. Though she likes to be fair and wonders if she is being unfair to Calum, she feels after consultation with Duror that she cannot have the brothers dictating to her.

After the fiasco of the deer hunt she is furious and wants the brothers removed from the wood, but decides to let them stay after Tulloch and Roderick have intervened and her brother is quite amenable to letting them remain. She is confronted with a less important decision about the two brothers later. Should she give them a lift back from Lendrick as Roderick is asking her to do, though her daughter Sheila opposes the idea? The lift is not given (113–14).

She often asks Duror about his wife and on one occasion brings her a bunch of chrysanthemums (134), though she finds the visit 'degrading' and 'shaming' since the fat, misshapen

Peggy insists on fawning rather slavishly on the lovely aristocrat. However, as a Christian, Lady Runcie-Campbell feels she ought to pay such visits.

Her husband, the absent Colin, a church-goer because that is expected of a laird, believes that there is some distinction of rank in heaven (136) but she herself finds such a belief 'impious'. She wishes her children to grow up and possess their inheritance but as the 'truly meek' (138).

In spite of her supposed Christianity, however, she is very angry when she finds the brothers in the beach hut even though they are sheltering from a fierce storm. She tells her children that she has never heard of such impertinence and agrees with her husband's view that after the war the lower classes are likely to be more demanding and presumptuous. There is a clear distinction in her mind between Roderick and the brothers. Roderick is to be protected from pneumonia. The brothers, however, in her opinion should be quite used to rain because of their job. She does not feel that she has done wrong in expelling them from the hut and tells Roderick that his sister has a far more mature attitude towards people of a lower class (172). One ought not to be arrogant and overbearing but at the same time one must keep a proper distance since one has a responsibility to society.

At the end of the book when Roderick climbs into the tree and cannot get down, she acts calmly and decisively, not panicking; yet her composure breaks at one point when she turns on Harry who, she thinks, has implied that Roderick is a coward. (In the aristocratic world the accusation of cowardice was an extreme insult. She thinks conventionally of the conscientious objectors as cowards though in fact the reason many of them would have objected to war and killing was because they were Christians like herself.) She decides that the cone-gatherers must be asked for help and sends Graham, who returns with the answer that she has to go and plead with the brothers herself. She finds the brothers' demand incomprehensible but decides to go. It is she who finds Calum's body. She goes down on her knees among the blood and the cones. She cannot pray but finds that she can weep and, as she weeps, pity and joy and hope well up in her heart. The fact that she had decided to go and see the brothers is a great concession for her and the ending shows that she has learnt a lesson about rank and Christianity.

She is a complex character. She is on her own during the war and has to make decisions. Often she turns to others for counsel and is not so inflexible that she will not change her mind. However, there is a conflict between rank and Christianity and she is often caught up in it. It is sad that Duror is the one she most often asks for guidance, especially in the light of his hatred of the brothers.

She is a not unlikeable character, caught between the ideas of her husband, Colin, on the one hand and those of her father, the judge, on the other.

Roderick

Roderick, son of Lady Runcie-Campbell, is, we are told, useless at games (36), awkward physically and mentally as far as sport is concerned. It may be that his clumsiness is partially responsible for his compassion for Calum. He had been from birth weak in body and is being tutored at home, having been removed from the rough and tumble of school.

He dislikes Duror since as an infant he had seen him with a dead roe deer (53). Nevertheless, he wishes to take part in the deer hunt and he perseveres in games though not good at them. He admires the brothers greatly for their daring agility in the trees.

From his grandfather, a judge, he has learnt a sense of fairness and justice and when his mother wants the brothers expelled after the deer hunt, he says that she is not being fair since Calum had not wanted to take part in the deer hunt in the first place. Similarly, he is ominously silent in the beach hut when his mother is again angry with the brothers. It is he who wants to give the brothers a lift from Lendrick. But his sister, Duror and his mother are opposed to him (114–15).

We are told that his grandfather was very fond of him (136–37) and had encouraged him to maintain a tenderness and sincerity towards inferiors.

The wood to him is partly a place of magical pilgrimage and terror, as if it was a wood in the Arthurian legends. We remember that the Arthurian knights had vowed to carry out good deeds. Once he sees Duror spying on the brothers' hut when he is bringing them a cake (144) and wonders why he hates the brothers so much and seeks to drive them out of the wood. 'Was it because they represented goodness, and himself [i.e. Duror] evil?' (145)

Why does he climb the tree at the end of the book? Clearly he is emulating the brothers and identifying with them since he is carrying a bag for cones. It may also be that he is finding events on the ground confusing with their unfairnesses and is seeking refuge in the trees. He is eventually rescued, though it is significant that he does not answer his mother when she shouts to him.

In summary, Roderick is not the typical son of a laird and does not hold his father's ideas. He is not good at sports. He treats the lower classes with sympathy and compassion. His moral ideas are derived more from his grandfather than from his father. He is a complete contrast to his sister who is an aristocratic and unfeeling snob. He dislikes Duror but admires the brothers. He is an imaginative boy whose heroes are Galahad (113, 145), and Christian in *The Pilgrim's Progress,* who represent the quest for moral goodness (142, 145).

Minor Characters

Dr Matheson seems to be rather a selfish person, thinking more about the personal inconveniences of war than of the deaths involved. He complains about the continual diet of Spam. When Duror brings him a gift of venison, he begins 'to dandle it, as if it was a new-born baby and he its delighted father' (117).

However, he is shrewd and, though he knows that nothing is wrong with Duror physically, he is not so sure that he is mentally healthy. Since Duror appears to have no religious faith he advises him that all he can do is endure his wife's infirmity, which, of course, he has been doing for a long time already (123–24). At this point, we feel a certain sympathy for Duror who, we discover, has only had three years of happily married life before his wife was stricken (124).

Mrs Lochie is Duror's mother-in-law. She looks after Peggy and the house in Duror's absence. Her habitual expression is one of 'dour resoluteness' (24). She is angry with God because of what has happened to her daughter (29). She accuses Duror of being fonder of his dogs than of his wife (31). As Neil wonders what would happen to Calum if he himself had an accident or fell ill, so Mrs Lochie wonders what will happen to Peggy if she is not there to take care of her (31). She seems to lead a dull life, looking after her daughter, listening to the wireless and knitting. We get the impression that she does not like her son-in-law much and she tells Lady Runcie-Campbell, in order to get him into trouble, that she has seen him with a doll and 'It's not got a stitch on' (179). Her personality and attitude clearly form part of Duror's wretchedly unhappy domestic circumstances.

Captain Forgan, Lady Runcie-Campbell's brother, is a typical upper-class type. It is he who asks for the deer hunt and we meet him first playing cricket with Roderick, his nephew (37). He is thirty-five years old and in peacetime a lawyer. When his sister is determined to get rid of the brothers after the fiasco of the deer hunt, she asks him for his opinion but he is not at all vindictive. He says that he bears Calum, whom he calls a 'poor fellow', no ill will (96). In sum, he is upper-class in his upbringing, is not ill-natured and has perhaps taken up the legal profession because his father was a judge.

Sheila Runcie-Campbell is what might be called a spoilt brat, the aristocracy at its worst. She objects to the brothers being given a lift back from Lendrick and says that her dog means more to her than they do (114). In the hut scene she giggles when Calum presents the wrong hand for the jacket that Neil is putting on him and she also draws attention to the holes in his pullover (158). She is the hard face of the upper-classes, spoilt, mocking, without compassion.

Peggy Duror is described physically as having 'great wobbling masses of pallid fat' (25). When she was younger, however, we are told that she had raced hand in hand with Duror through whins and briers. She talks in an almost 'simple' fashion and dandles her pillow as if it was a baby. She is haunted by her earlier days and, according to her mother, was once happy and made others happy too (28). However, Lady Runcie-Campbell does not like visiting her because she fawns on her and 'simpers' since she is upper-class. She is a miserable person whose life is tedious and regretful, and Duror no longer loves her.

Mrs Morton, the housekeeper at the Big House, is a sensible cheerful buxom widow (41). She visits Peggy regularly; she thinks Duror 'distinguished' (43). In speaking to her, Duror shows the coarse side of his nature and would marry her if Peggy were no longer alive. Duror lies to her about Calum's supposed indecency (47) but she tells him that he must not become embittered (48).

Mr Tulloch represents one of the indubitably good influences in the book. He is the forester at Ardmore where the brothers usually work. He tells Lady Runcie-Campbell that Calum has scruples about the deer hunt (59–60) and that he has already excluded the brothers from deer hunts at Ardmore. He understands Calum and says that his behaviour at the hunt was not his fault (94, 96). It is possible that his sympathy and compassion may arise from his own acquaintance with grief since his brother was killed at Dunkirk (164). He tries to be fair to Lady Runcie-Campbell, but because of her hostility to the brothers he decides to take them back to Ardmore and replace them with conscientious objectors (165) whom he does not dislike though, as has been said, his own brother has been killed in the war. Indeed, he tries to help these conscientious objectors by washing the graffiti from their huts at Ardmore, graffiti which say that they are 'yellow-bellies' (189). He recognises Duror's hatred for the brothers and tries to find an explanation. In short, he is an example of fairness and compassion and goodness, and a good friend to the brothers.

There remain Harry, the apprentice gardener, old Graham, the handyman, and Betty, the gum-chewing land girl. They represent ordinary human beings who at times lighten the action by humour, Graham tending to be a moaner, Betty, a Glaswegian, fond of songs, and Harry a player of the mouth organ.

6. THE MORAL QUESTION

Many books are written for entertainment alone, but the best books are those which deal with moral questions, that is, issues of right and wrong and good and evil. This book does not simply tell a story: it deals with the eternal war between goodness on the one side and evil on the other.

Various reasons are given for Duror's hatred for Calum: for instance, Calum releases rabbits from the traps Duror has set (7). Also the hatred may be instinctive, such as that which animals feel for a 'freak', one that is not like themselves. Again, Calum's ugly body may remind Duror of his wife. However, we feel that perhaps such reasons are not enough and that in some sense Duror represents the forces of evil and Calum the forces of innocence. Indeed, the wood may remind us of the Garden of Eden, with Duror skulking about in it, like the devil, spying on the two brothers. Calum seems entirely innocent of rancour or hatred of any kind, even though he has much to be embittered about. He has a simple, childlike faith in heaven.

We have already said that, by setting his scene against a background of the Second World War, Jenkins gained an extra dimension for his novel. During the Second World War the German nation was led by a dictator, Adolf Hitler, who had a pathological hatred of the Jews. He believed that the Jews were an inferior race and the German or Aryan race a master race. For this reason, Jews were put into concentration camps and systematically murdered in what became known as the Holocaust. Jews had been persecuted before but there had been no attempt to wipe them out completely as Hitler was determined to do. Homosexuals, too, were to be destroyed, as were the handicapped. In this sense, Duror's attitude may be likened to that of a Nazi towards a Jew.

Calum, on the other hand, seems essentially good: his attitude to the world is one of open trust. Yet this trust is abused by Duror, who lies about him (saying he is a pervert) and puts him at a disadvantage (as in the deer hunt). He wants to drive him out of the wood at all costs. Therefore, one of the main questions in the book is: 'Can absolute goodness survive in our world?' Or rather 'why does evil exist?'

In this book there are references to the policy of murdering the Jews. We learn that he, Duror, had

> [...] read that the Germans were putting idiots and cripples to death in gas chambers. Outwardly, as everybody expected, he condemned such barbarity; inwardly, thinking of idiocy and crippledness not as abstractions but as embodied in the crouch-backed cone-gatherer, he had profoundly approved. (15)

Later, we read, with regard to Neil, 'They were not Jews being dragged to the concentration camp' (100).

We have, therefore, to remember that one of the strengths of the book is the deeper dimension given it by the war. There is evil in the wood but also evil represented by the war outside the wood. Many people were sacrificed to destroy the evil of Nazism, including Tulloch's brother (164). Calum was sacrificed before Duror killed himself (219). It is an interesting point that Hitler himself probably committed suicide in the bunker in which he and his minions entrenched themselves at the end.

7. THE RELIGIOUS ASPECT

Apart from the central struggle between good and evil to which we have referred, there are other religious references to which attention might be drawn.

Firstly, the idyllic nature of the wood might remind us of the Garden of Eden into which evil is introduced to destroy the innocent. Duror wishes to expel Neil and Calum from the 'garden'. Secondly, we may think of the episode in which the brothers are expelled from the hut by Lady Runcie-Campbell as reminiscent of the 'No room at the inn' scene in the Bible.[3] Thirdly, the relationship of Neil to Calum might remind us of the phrase in the Bible, 'Am I my brother's keeper?'[4] Finally, when we visualise Calum's body hanging in the tree we may think of the Crucifixion:

> He hung [...] in twisted fashion, and kept swinging. His arms were loose and dangled in macabre gestures of supplication. (219)

According to Christian belief, of course, the Crucifixion is not a death without hope, but was intended to happen, and mankind would be saved by means of it. Like Christ, Calum is innocent and his death is, therefore, a sacrifice which in some way is to help men. The other elements of hope are the cones which drip down with the blood and are symbols of renewal and regeneration.

All these elements remain at the back of our minds, suggestive symbols which hover over the action and give it religious depth.

Apart from these elements, there are also direct references to God. Thus, in conversation with Duror, Mrs Lochie says that Mary Black has told her that what happened to Peggy was punishment from God. But she says that she told Mary Black that she would question God to His very face (28–29). She would ask Him what right He had to punish the innocent. Certainly, pain and illness, and in this case deformity, might well raise questions about God's dealings with people. Duror himself is not religious, and it may be that it is because of his wife's deformity that he is not.

Mrs Morton tells Duror, who has been trying to poison her mind about the brothers and especially Calum:

> "There's nothing known to their discredit, if that's what you mean, John. It's true the small one's not as God meant a man to be; but that's God's business, not ours." (46)

We might gather from this that Mrs Morton is a believer who is willing to leave the conduct of the world to God, except for a little remark she makes to Roderick:

> "No harm will come to you, laddie," she said, "if God looks after His own. If," she added, turning away. (141)

In the mind and soul of Lady Runcie-Campbell there is a struggle between her feudal ideas of rank and her Christianity. She tries to act in accordance with her Christian ideals by, for instance, visiting Duror's wife even though she finds her revolting. But at the same time her Christian ideals are undermined by the burden of her aristocratic beliefs. She acts by her instinctive ideas of rank when she forces Calum into the deer hunt and cannot understand how he can have the impudence to refuse. She sees no conflict between her belief in Christianity and the slaughter of deer. She puts the brothers out of the hut and she commands them at the end of the book to come and rescue her son from the tree.

When she is demanding, after the deer hunt, that they be dismissed from the wood, she is reminded by Tulloch of Christianity when he says that he has questioned the brothers and says he can 'find no fault in them' (94). These are the words used by Pilate, the Roman governor who had Christ crucified, with the simple substitution of 'them' for 'Him'.[5] However, she does not seem to hear what Tulloch is saying to her.

Lady Runcie-Campbell's beliefs are explained in the following way:

> If she had not altogether inherited her religion from her father, certainly it had been much influenced by him. Accustomed to seeing humanity in its most vicious aspects, he had been uncompromising, imperturbable, and ironical in his Christianity. For the Church as an institution he had often expressed a distrust all the more effective for being so judicially delivered. Towards Colin, as a typical master of that Church, with his own feudal enclosure in the local kirk, he had been similarly tolerant but distrustful. (136)

Thus, she had been influenced by her father who as a judge had to learn to be fair, who was also a Christian but not overfond of the Church. Her husband, Colin, on the other hand, was a Christian only because as a laird he had to set a good example. Her father was a charitable Christian whose views were represented by a verse which he liked from an old ballad:

> If meat and drink thou never gavest nane,
> Every night and all,
> The fire will burn thee to the bare bane,
> And Christ receive thy saule. (136)

Thus, Lady Runcie-Campbell is torn between her religious belief and her rank, and it is only at the end that she breaks free from her sense of rank in order to save her son and goes to plead with the brothers.

Her son, Roderick, has in fact inherited a sense of fairness and Christian charity from his grandfather. He protests to his mother when she is going to dismiss the brothers from the wood after the deer hunt (94), and he is angry when she puts them out of the beach hut (158–60). He identifies himself with the brothers by climbing the tree with his bag for cones. (His sister, on the other hand, is nastily assured in her aristocratic rank and shows no charity at all.)

Perhaps because of the struggle he has had with looking after Calum, we learn that Neil has no belief in the afterlife. When Calum says during the storm that he can see the light of heaven in which his mother now is, Neil says that he himself has no belief in heaven. Calum, however, has a childlike belief (149–50).

Questions, therefore, are raised throughout the book about God and about His justice. Why was Peggy misshapen? Why was Calum deformed? Calum himself shows no bitterness. Duror does, and Neil also does to a certain extent.

To sum up: Mrs Lochie questions God's justice; Lady Runcie-Campbell sways between her Christian belief and her ingrained ideas of rank; her father the judge believed that goodness would eventually win the battle; the absent laird is a conventional churchgoer; Roderick has a fine sense of fairness and sees himself sometimes in the middle of a story about Arthurian knights (of whom Sir Galahad was the most virtuous). Duror, of course, is no believer, which is why the doctor tells him that all he can do is 'endure' his wife's illness.

8. CLASS

Undoubtedly, one of the themes in the book is that of class. In the upper-classes, we have the absent laird, Sir Colin; his wife, Lady Runcie-Campbell; her brother, Captain Forgan; her son and daughter, Roderick and Sheila. Matheson, as a doctor, would be middle-class. The rest of the people in the book would probably be characterised as lower-class, including of course Neil and Calum, Duror and his wife and mother-in-law, Tulloch and the other employees such as Graham, Harry, Betty, and Mrs Morton.

We do not see much of Captain Forgan but his ideals seem aristocratic. It is he who wants the deer hunt, though, of course, his sister has nothing against the sport. We also see him playing cricket with his nephew. Normally, Roderick would be in a public school except that it is considered that there would be too much rough and tumble for him, and he is a rather delicate boy.

Sir Colin, we gather, is a typical laird. As such, he has his family enclosure in the local church. He thinks the ordinary people are quite different from the upper-classes. He says:

> "What d'you expect, Elizabeth? They're still brutes under the skin, y'know. [...] After the war they'll be trying to drag us down to their level. It's up to us to see they don't manage it." (198)

He also believes, according to his wife, that there is a class structure in heaven; she as a Christian cannot agree with this (136). One imagines him as a typical laird, representative of his class, rather unthinking. His daughter would be close to him in her feudal ideas. His son Roderick seems to have been greatly influenced by his grandfather who has made more allowances for him than his father did (136–37). Probably because he was not good at sports and was rather delicate, his father would be a bit disappointed in him.

While Sir Colin sees the war as a threat to the class structure, Neil sees it as hope for the common man (154). He believes that after the war there will be radical changes and that Lady

Runcie-Campbell will not be able to treat Calum and himself in the way she does. He resents the fact that she lives in a mansion with a large number of rooms while he and Calum inhabit a squalid hut (4).

We have already discussed how Lady Runcie-Campbell sways between her instinctive ideas about rank and her Christianity. In general, her feudal beliefs are victorious till the very end of the book. She does not wish to give the brothers a lift back from Lendrick (113), although later she feels remorse for this (135). And we have already discussed her conflicts with them. She does try at times to be fair and it is probable that her husband would have had no hesitation in dismissing the brothers after the fiasco of the deer hunt. It may be said in her defence that she is acting on behalf of her husband who is in the war and that this will make her divided and over-anxious, but in the end one must admit that over the whole book her ideas about rank prevail. In fact, it may be that the author is raising the question whether rank and Christianity can be reconciled at all.

9. NATURE

By setting the novel in a wood, the author is permitted to write about nature and the links between man and nature in a way that gives depth to the book.

Though nature can be beautiful, it can also be cruel. Animals prey on each other, but man adds to the cruelty by killing for sport as in the deer hunt. Deer, which to the rest of us are lovely elegant animals, are considered by Duror to be 'vermin'. Calum knows that an owl must kill voles (3), but that it does so for food and survival. Man, however, kills for sport and causes unnecessary pain. Duror does this with his rabbit traps.

Their attitude to nature sometimes defines the characters. Duror is needlessly cruel and even his dogs are afraid of him. He fantasises about whipping them till the blood comes (34) and his behaviour during the deer hunt is barbaric (86). Calum, however, suffers with the suffering animals: he tries to free the rabbits from their traps and thus antagonises Duror (7–8). He runs with the fleeing deer as if he himself were a victim (84–85). Neil, however, considers nature to be hostile. Roderick thinks of the wood as an enchanted place which can also be frightening. Calum is perfectly at home in the wood. Neil worries whether he himself might have an accident, in which case there will be no one to look after Calum (64). Nature can erupt in lightning and thunder and cause the brothers trouble with Lady Runcie-Campbell when they break into the beach hut. At one stage Duror has a nightmare of his wife being attacked by thrushes (77).

People are also compared to animals. Calum is compared to a monkey (56, 78), and like a monkey he is at home in the trees. The doctor is compared by Duror to a 'greedy old pig' (22). Roderick has a 'deer's eyes and hare's teeth' (37). Lady Runcie-Campbell tells Tulloch that the brothers are being 'as discreet as squirrels' (57). Calum is compared to a 'dog in the presence of someone who has been cruel to it' (67). Neil objects to himself and his brother being treated like 'dogs' (72). Betty's laughter is compared to a 'hyena's' (83). Neil decides after the deer hunt that they should keep out of the way like insects, 'not bees or ants which could sting and bite, but tiny flies which could do no harm since there was nothing in creation so feeble as not to be able to molest them' (98–99). The doctor tells Duror when he is examining him that he is 'sound as an ox' (121). In the pub scene Calum is by implication compared to an ape (131–32). After Graham's tiring journey in search of the brothers 'he had to sit on the ground, peching like a seal' (207).

On the one hand, man is part of nature, but on the other is set apart from it. Duror, though a gamekeeper, is not really in harmony with it; he projects his own unhappiness and cruelty on it. Thus, at one point he thinks it is his wife, not the deer, that he is attacking with a knife (86–87). In his treatment of rabbits he is more cruel than nature itself (8–9). Calum finds man's cruelty tormenting. In his leisure time he carves representations of animals with marvellous fidelity (192). As far as Neil is concerned, Lady Runcie-Campbell loves her dogs more than she loves human beings and, in fact, Sheila, her daughter, says this quite bluntly (114).

Actually, Calum is quite defenceless and without Neil to protect him would probably not survive as long as some of the animals.

The cones are a very powerful symbol in the book. They represent the resurrection of the wood after the war is over.

Outside the wood men are fighting and killing each other on a much larger scale than animals ever do, while the Nazis are trying to exterminate another part of the human race (the Jews) which, of course, animals would never do. Even the trees themselves can be considered victims of the war.

By comparing Calum to a monkey who is perfectly happy in the trees but not on the ground, the author may be saying that the troubles of mankind began when they came down from the trees.

In general, human beings are here seen as the most cruel of animals.

10. THE ENDING OF THE BOOK

Some might find the ending of the book puzzling. Calum has been killed and Duror has committed suicide. Yet Lady Runcie-Campbell, while kneeling down among the blood and the spilt cones, wept, 'and as she wept pity, and purified hope, and joy welled up in her heart' (220).

Where does this hope come from, or this joy? It cannot surely come from the death of Calum. After all, his life has not been a fortunate one, though he has not shown bitterness.

The case is rather complicated and to understand it we must think of Calum not simply as a person but as a symbol. What, therefore, does Calum symbolise in the book? In the first place, he seems to symbolise goodness. Duror sees him as partly monstrous but also as having a beautiful angelic face (12). His brother, Neil, thinks that he is the best of human beings (153). He seems entirely innocent and without malice.

He, therefore, appears a Christ-like figure. Christ, too, was innocent, without malice and without bitterness. Christ, too, did not repel violence with more violence. Christ, in spite of this, was crucified. And Calum's position in the tree as described at the end looks like a crucifixion (219).

Christ's crucifixion was not an end but a beginning. By means of it, men and women were forgiven their sins. His crucifixion was a symbol of hope. He paid for the sins of human beings with His own death.

It must be that Lady Runcie-Campbell saw Calum not as a simple human being but as a Christ-like symbol and this explains her 'hope' and 'joy'.

Whether, however, Calum can take on himself the weight of a Christ is dubious. After all, he is not, as Christ was, the Son of God. Unlike Christ, he was a retarded human being. Nor can Duror be seen simply as a Judas. After all, Judas was one of Christ's disciples and Duror hated Calum from the beginning. It is also possible that it was not just Calum's death that made Duror kill himself: his life, such as it was, was wretched and miserable.

Thus, it may be that the reader will find the ending unsatisfactory. The novelist may be putting too much weight on

Calum's death as a symbol for renewal as well as on the cones as a similar symbol.

It is for readers to make their own mind up about the ending. It may be that for some readers the ending will appear entirely satisfactory and a solution to the events that have preceded it. Or is the author perhaps saying that Calum's death has not been in vain since it has so profoundly affected Lady Runcie-Campbell?

One of the pleasures of reading good novels is that these questions can be argued. There is no set answer as in mathematics and each reader can bring to the book his or her knowledge and experience.

11. THE NOVEL AS FABLE

Because of the simplicity of the structure of the novel and its atmosphere, *The Cone-Gatherers* has been compared to a fable, though generally, as in Aesop's *Fables,* such stories are about animals such as foxes and hens, and there is a moral at the end. An extended form of fable is *Animal Farm* which is about animals and in which George Orwell was teaching a moral about political power, among other things.

The fact that this novel is for the most part set in a wood suggests a certain simplicity. It deals with essentials which might be disguised if, for instance, it were a novel set in a busy town.

The number of characters of importance is very small and these react with each other in a fairly confined space. It is true that there is a scene in Lendrick but the action is set mostly in the wood.

The fact, too, that Neil and particularly Calum are so at home in the trees suggests that they are almost like animals and, indeed, Calum is described in terms of a monkey or an ape (78–79). There is one particular section which is very interesting, where Roderick is travelling through the wood in search of the brothers in order to give them a cake. The wood to him is a place of magic and terror. It

> [...] was enchanted, full of terrifying presences. [...] Low-hanging branches were evil birds swooping with talons ready to rip his face and pluck out his eyes. (143)

It reminds him of the knight Sir Galahad and of Christian in John Bunyan's *The Pilgrim's Progress* (142). These people were often to encounter evil beings, just as he was shortly to see Duror.

It is often possible, too, to think of a wood as a place where we might get easily lost, where the way is not clear, and in this wood the way is not clear sometimes for Roderick, or his mother, or the two brothers.

We have already discussed the moral that we get from this book. It seems to be about good and evil and how good, though destroyed in the person of Calum, still seems to give a reason for hope.

It is possible, too, to think of Duror as an animal whose helpless prey is Calum and who may be attracted into murder by Calum's very weakness.

Most fables such as those of Aesop are set in a rural environment. For example a fox or some other animal may be tricked by its own reflection in a pool or it may be tricked into speaking and, therefore, losing a hen that it has in its mouth. The background here, of course, is also one of nature and though the participants are human beings and not animals, they are often compared to animals as we have seen already. Thus, in the same way as Duror traps the rabbit, so he sets a trap for Calum by means of the deer hunt. Later, as he kills the rabbit, he kills Calum.

In general, therefore, the comparative brevity of the book, the setting and the uncomplicated structure, as well as the atmosphere, make this book appear like a fable, though perhaps the animal in human beings, as represented by Duror, seems to be worse than any of the actual animals mentioned in the novel.

12. FURTHER READING

Robin Jenkins has written over twenty novels, but we will select here only two for special mention.

The Changeling

The first one is *The Changeling*, which is set for the most part in Argyll in the area of Dunoon. It begins, however, in Glasgow. The two most important characters in the book are an unpromoted teacher called Charlie Forbes who teaches in a Glasgow school, and a pupil, Tom Curdie, who is thirteen years old and, though he comes from a very deprived area, is intelligent enough to be in a top academic class. His mother is fat and lazy and she lives with Shoogle Kemp, described as 'of no account'.[6] The environment could not be worse – rough and filthy; and Tom has a younger brother and sister whom he has to look after.

Tom is streetwise and, among other things, a thief. He steals from teachers in the school, including Charlie Forbes himself, though the latter does not know it till the end of the book. Forbes has a fairly kind attitude towards the pupils of the school and does not like unjust accusations or severe punishment. However, because he is unpromoted he has little influence and is laughed at by more cynical senior staff. He recognises Tom's intelligence and decides, with his wife's reluctant approval, to take the boy on holiday with his family (Charlie himself, his wife Mary, daughter Gillian, son Alistair and well-off mother-in-law, Mrs Storrock) to Towellan, which is not far from Dunroth (probably Dunoon).

The entry of Tom, or the changeling, into the family sets up problems which a more intelligent man than Charlie Forbes might have foreseen. His wife accuses him of being more favourable to Tom than to his own children, and Gillian, in particular, dislikes the newcomer. She thinks him 'sleekit', that is sly, and intent on ingratiating himself with her father. A particular incident causes a serious rift in the family. Gillian sees Tom steal from Woolworths articles which in fact are of no earthly use to him. On the other hand, he pays money over the counter for a brooch for Mrs Forbes.

What Gillian does not realise is that Tom is feeling so comfortable with the family that he forgets sometimes that he is not going to be with them permanently. His theft, therefore, is merely a way of establishing in his own mind that he will have to return to a very different environment at the end of the holiday.

Gillian, of course, is too young to realise this and tells her mother about the theft. When she in turn tells Charlie he seems to think that Gillian, who has consistently disliked Tom, is making the story up. Gillian sees how difficult this is for her father to accept and says that her story about the theft was a lie. Obviously, these strains cannot be good for the family.

Young friends of Tom, members of his 'gang', come to the area and live there in a tent. One in particular follows Tom about as if he wishes to tell him something, but Tom refuses to speak to him. Then his slatternly mother and her equally inadequate partner come to visit Tom with the other two children. At one point they seem to be trying to blackmail Forbes as a homosexual because of his friendship with Tom. Tom is now utterly confused. He no longer knows where his home is. He does not want to go back to his deprived 'home' in Glasgow: he has seen an alternative world of great beauty and has known some humane people.

At this point two policemen come to the Forbes's cottage. Tom's friends have been caught stealing and the policemen think that Tom is the mastermind behind them. Gillian, who has now changed her mind about Tom owing to a deeper perception of his character, takes him away to a hut. And there, while she is outside, Tom, totally confused by the events that have happened to him, kills himself.

Superficially, this book is quite different from *The Cone-Gatherers,* but there is the same emphasis on good and evil. Was Charlie Forbes right in taking Tom on holiday? Did he think the enterprise through? Did he realise that by doing so he would be exposing Tom to an environment in which he would be much happier? At one time without thinking about it, Tom refers to himself as Tom Forbes. Then we might ask why Charlie Forbes had invited him on holiday at all. Was it to appease his own social conscience? Was it perhaps in order to use his kindness as a lever to get promotion, in order to show that he was a caring teacher? Thus, the concept of 'goodness' is examined in the person of Charlie Forbes. Acts which may appear good may have terrible consequences. Had he been thinking more about himself than about Tom in his act of supposed kindness? And so on.

Both books end with a death. Both Duror and Tom have come to an impossible barrier; the only way round it seems to be suicide. Again, the environment for the most part in the two books is the beautiful west coast of Scotland, contrasted in this book with appallingly ugly areas of Glasgow. The author knows Glasgow well since from 1936 to 1940 he taught English in a Glasgow school. After the Second World War, which concluded in 1945, he again took up teaching in Glasgow, being appointed to a post in a 'deprived area' of the city. During the war years, of course, he was as we know a conscientious objector working for the Forestry Commission in Argyll. In 1955 he moved back to a teaching job in Dunoon. This book was first published in 1958.

Thus, this novel also shows a moral question being set up and analysed. Should Charlie Forbes have taken Tom on holiday? And having committed himself to Tom, should he have stuck to him through thick and thin, for by the end of the book he says that he has found him 'sly, secretive, and deceitful, and not the kind of companion we like for our own children' (182). The lesson of the book appears to be that we should not interfere in other people's lives unless we know exactly what we are doing. Tom needed total commitment and this Forbes was not prepared to give. In the absence of such commitment, his so-called 'kindness' and 'goodness' led to a tragedy.

The Thistle and the Grail

The second book which you might find interesting is called *The Thistle and the Grail.* This book is a story about football and a particular club called Drumsagart Thistle, which is a Junior team. It has had a succession of bad results till two players are introduced, one a defender in his thirties, and the other, a young free-scoring centre forward. However, the book, though it has some descriptions of games, is really not so much about football as about its supporters.

Football is shown as almost a religion and religious terms such as 'martyrs' (the club's football supporters in its bad days), 'canonised' and 'saints' are used in descriptions of it. The Grail is a term used for the Scottish Junior Cup and is itself a religious symbol, being the cup in which Christ's blood was collected after the Crucifixion. The Thistle, of course, in the title of the novel, refers to the club.

Football is also what gives meaning to the lives of the spectators, some of whom are old. Thus, one of them says that if the team wins the Scottish Junior Cup, he would die happy. Football generates such intensity of devotion that the father who has lost his daughter goes to a match the day of her funeral. And there are a number of episodes where ordinary human feeling can be eroded in the thirst for victory. There is, however, a sergeant of police in the book who keeps insisting that football is only a game and that human beings are more important than it.

Football is also associated with historical defeats; when the team loses by eight goals to nil, one of the characters says that it is worse than Flodden (a battle in which the Scots were thoroughly defeated by the English in 1513).

It is, on the whole, a book with a masculine atmosphere. Women, in general, are treated with contempt and, indeed, one of them is physically beaten. The novel, which was published in 1954, shows men trying to escape the ugliness of their environment in the dream of winning the Scottish Junior Cup.

The number of characters is larger than in the other two books mentioned, and the author handles them with confidence and a good knowledge of their modes of speech. There is also more humour in this book than in the other two, as one might expect in a novel about football.

As one would also expect from Jenkins, there is a moral dimension to the book. It is not just in the comparison of football with religious fervour; as we have already seen, religious speculations occur often in his books. What we have here is the idea that even with a goal in itself worth aiming for, as this club aims for the Scottish Junior title, there will, simply because we are human beings, always be corruption. And this is shown in the person of Andrew Rutherford, president of the club. He is a man who tries to be generous and honourable but whose motives and actions are misunderstood and questioned, even by his own father who believes that the brotherhood of man will be set up on earth and who has perhaps unrealistic ideals. However, when after his father's death Andrew has occasion to believe that his father has perhaps as a councillor taken bribes, he becomes himself corrupt and uses unworthy methods to bring about the replay of a game which Drumsagart lost. There is in fact a Judas in the book who betrays his own brother to Rutherford and, when the latter gets the information, he refuses to pay the money he promised. As always, the central idea is goodness. How can it survive in a corrupt world? Calum, Charlie Forbes, Andrew Rutherford – of these Calum is the only one who appears absolutely good. The other two fail the test. It is only in the joy of victory that the author finds salvation in *The Thistle and The Grail*. Rutherford's fierce wife sees on her husband's face and hears in his voice after the Cup has been won an innocent and spontaneous joy:

> Rutherford sat amidst that busload of familiar men, noticing how happiness had purged them, as it had purged him, of all his characteristic meanness and selfishness. This really was how men were, how they would wish to be always if circumstances allowed them.[7]

But Rutherford who had stuck with the team has to leave Drumsagart because his wife wishes to live in Helensburgh, a more pleasant environment, and a more upper-class one. Jenkins's characters never quite obtain that happiness and goodness which they sometimes glimpse, except only Calum who was retarded and, therefore, not quite capable of understanding and fully participating in a corrupt world.

13. REFERENCES

1. Introduction to *The Cone-Gatherers*, p.viii, editor Barry Pateman, Longman, Harlow 1991.
2. Introduction to *The Cone-Gatherers*, p.vi, editor Barry Pateman, Longman, Harlow 1991.
3. Luke, 2:7
4. Genesis, 4:9
5. Luke, 23:4; John, 18:38; 19:4; 19:6
6. Page references to *The Changeling* are to the Canongate Classics edition, Edinburgh 1989.
7. *The Thistle and The Grail*, p. 289, Scottish Fiction Reprint Library edition, Paul Harris Publishing, Edinburgh 1983.

14. QUESTIONS

The Cone-Gatherers

1. This novel is set during the Second World War. What advantages does the novelist derive from this?

2. How does the idea of 'class distinction' figure in the novel?

3. Examine carefully the section relating to the brothers' visit to Lendrick. What is the attitude of the villagers to them?

4. Though Colin, Lady Runcie-Campbell's husband, does not actually appear in the novel, his ideas are important to his wife. What are these ideas and how do they affect her behaviour?

5. What is the significance of the 'storm scene'?

6. What do you think of the novel's ending? Are you happy with it?

7. Duror represents the force of evil in the novel. What characters represent the force of good?

8. Look at the section in which the minor characters are listed. What do any three of them contribute to the novel?

9. Why does Neil refuse to help Lady Runcie-Campbell? Do you think he is right or wrong?

10. Is it possible to feel any sympathy for Duror or is he a monster that one cannot understand?

11. Study the deer hunt sequence carefully. Show the difference between Calum and Duror at this point.

15. NOTES ON *THE CONE-GATHERERS*

Page references are to the 2012 Canongate edition

p. 9, line 9	**thrawn** – stubborn
p. 10, line 7	**bothy** – hut
p. 18, line 13	**national service** – service for one's country, usually in the armed forces in wartime, but sometimes in such occupations as forestry
p. 24, line 4	**wireless set** – radio. There would be no TV at this time. Wireless sets were usually large and run on batteries
p. 27, line 17	**'The Rowan Tree'** – a Scottish song
p. 27, line 22	**Stalingrad** – the unsuccessful and prolonged siege of the Russian city by the Germans was a turning point in the war
p. 29, line 29	**wean** – child
p. 38, line 23	**African desert** – the North African desert was a major theatre of war, where General Montgomery inflicted a decisive defeat on Rommel, the German general, at El Alamein
p. 39, line 27	**Home Guard** – a volunteer force for home defence, first used in the Second World War
p. 45, line 9	**gean tree** – the wild cherry
p. 55, line 15	**beaters** – people employed to rouse game for others to shoot at
p. 57, line 17	**wizard** – magical, wonderful
p. 58, line 1	**quid pro quo** – something in return for something given
p. 59, line 16	**conscientious objectors** – those who refuse to fight in a war, often on religious grounds
p. 63, line 9	**tocher** – dowry
p. 75, line 1	**Cupid** – the god of Love
p. 86, line 23	**glaikit** – foolish
p. 89, line 27	**huff** – a fit of anger or sulks
p. 90, line 18	**oxter** – armpit
p. 93, line 7	**shooting-brake** – an estate car
p. 94, line 25	**Pilate** – the Roman governor who had Christ crucified
p. 102, line 14	**grue** – shudder
p. 105, line 21	**rations** – the amount of food and clothes available to one person were restricted during the war and they were awarded on a coupon system
p. 107, line 11	**byke** – nest
p. 107, line 28	**tholing** – enduring
p. 113, line 24	**Sir Galahad** – one of the knights of the Round Table, famous for his courtesy

p. 120, line 14	**saps** – a mixture of bread and tea (or milk)
p. 120, line 26	**mak siccar** – make sure
p. 120, line 29	**a staunch Kirk hand** – a regular church-goer
p. 121, line 7	**Beelzebub** – a devil
p. 122, line 5	**Lord Byron** – a famous nineteenth-century poet, well-known for his good looks
p. 124, line 7	**scunners** – sickens
p. 124, line 8	**godmongers** – dealers in religion
p. 125, line 15	**Hercules** – the physically very strong Greek hero was tricked by Atlas, who held the world on his back, to take over the burden
p. 130, line 28	**ATS** – Auxiliary Territorial Service, replaced by the Women's Royal Auxiliary Corps in 1949
p. 133, line 15	**Mull** – an island off the west coast of Scotland
p. 142, line 13	**land girl** – one who did her national service by working on the land
p. 142, line 27	**Christian** – the hero of *The Pilgrim's Progress,* famous book by John Bunyan (1628–1688)
p. 151, line 28	**forby** – as well as that
p. 165, line 22	**drooking** – drenching
p. 206, line 7	**Sargasso** – a floating mass of seaweed in the Western Atlantic

SCOTNOTES

Study guides to major Scottish writers and literary texts

Produced by the Education Committee
of the Association for Scottish Literary Studies

THE ASSOCIATION FOR SCOTTISH LITERARY STUDIES aims to promote the study, teaching and writing of Scottish literature, and to further the study of the languages of Scotland.

To these ends, the ASLS publishes works of Scottish literature; literary criticism and in-depth reviews of Scottish books in *Scottish Literary Review*; short articles, features and news in *ScotLit*; and scholarly studies of language in *Scottish Language*. It also publishes *New Writing Scotland*, an annual anthology of new poetry, drama and short fiction, in Scots, English and Gaelic. ASLS has also prepared a range of teaching materials covering Scottish language and literature for use in schools.

All the above publications are available as a single 'package', in return for an annual subscription. Enquiries should be sent to:

ASLS
Scottish Literature
7 University Gardens
University of Glasgow
Glasgow G12 8QH

Tel/fax +44 (0)141 330 5309
e-mail **office@asls.org.uk**
or visit our website at **www.asls.org.uk**